Towhead and the Fireworks

Helen L. Merrell
Rita K. Fisher

To order additional copies of this book, contact:
Xlibris
1-888-795-4274
www.Xlibris.com
Orders@Xlibris.com

ISBN: Softcover   978-1-7960-9298-1
        EBook   978-1-7960-9297-4

Print information available on the last page

Rev. date: 03/13/2020

This book is dedicated to my daughter Rita K. Fisher for all of her love and kindness and care for me through all these years.

I must give many thanks to my dearest friend, Lynn Flint for all the time, friendship, patients, and love that she has given me, so I can try to make my books perfect. Thank you my Dear.

Towhead and his family we're getting ready for the once-a-year fun time celebration. It was the Fourth of July picnic. While Towhead was helping dad set up the picnic table alongside the driveway he asked Towhead if he knew what the Declaration of Independence was. Towhead said yes, teacher taught us that in school. It was the thirteen colonies that wrote the Declaration that gave the people the freedom to worship their own way. And to live the way we wanted to live. Father said, aren't you glad we have our freedoms?.

Father was placing picnic tables in the driveway, while Mother place red white and blue tablecloth on them. As friends and neighbors were bringing well filled baskets of food. The picnic tables were loaded with pies, cakes, salads, and lots of mouth-watering fried chicken. The boys were playing on the basketball court that Dad had built for Towhead, while the girls were playing fetch with Sammy, and badminton in the yard.

The music in the background had everyone humming along with the familiar patriotic songs they all knew. And you would hear Kate Smith belt out God Bless America and you just had to join in singing too. It kept everyone in a happy mood. The men were exchanging stories of the wars they had served in and they all said they were thankful for their freedom.

As time begin to fade into evening, everybody complain that they ate too much and how good everything was, they were anxious for the fireworks to begin. The mothers reminded the children to be careful with the hot wires and then they were given sparkler to enjoy. Dad finally brought out the fireworks. Everyone got excited. They waited for the loud boom Banner the pretty lights in the sky.

When the noisy celebration began Sammy hid under a table in the driveway. Everyone oohed and aahed. They enjoyed all the bright colors in the sky and didn't want the evening to end. After the fireworks were over, tables with cleaned up and put away. It was then they realized that Sammy was no longer there. Towhead became very upset and Mother had to convince him that Sammy would be found. Everyone started going in different directions looking and calling, but Sammy was nowhere to be found. After few hours the search party broke up. Young ones started to return to their homes but promised to be back in the morning to see if Sammy had returned. They would decided if Sammy had not come home during the night, that the search would continue again in the morning. While the older folks kept searching.

Towhead did not want to go to bed. He was remembering have Santa Claus had brought her to him one Christmas as a special Christmas gift.

He was crying now, mother put her arms around him and said don't worry son she's someplace and we will find her. The search party continued and mother told towhead he needed to rest and told him she would wake him when they had some news.

Towhead said "Okay Mom, but I want to take one more look in the barn maybe Sammy went there to get away from the noise and bright lights."

Towhead was just about to go to the barn when he heard a dog barking he looked out to the field and that's when he saw Sammy he started running to her. He fell to the ground and Sammy fell into his lap. NOh Sammy I'm so glad to see you, where have you been?" Sammy was kissing Towhead all over his face, he finally said "that's enough Sammy I don't need a bath".

Mother and Dad saw what was happening and went to help get Sammy into the house. "Let's get Sammy some warm blankets and give her some water and some warm milk she needs a bath but that can wait until morning" said mother "well, we need to shower her with some love right now".

Towhead placed Sammy on the foot of his bed he couldn't quit petting her. Then Towhead knelt beside his bed to say his prayers and thank God for loving Sammy enough to let her come home. He asked for a blessing for his mother and his dad and everyone who helped look for. Sammy and said "please God don't let Sammy run away again. I love her so much amen".

The End

Printed in the United States
By Bookmasters